# Momma, Will You?

by **Dori Chaconas**

*paintings by*
**Steve Johnson** and **Lou Fancher**

VIKING

Momma, will you feed the hen?
Yes or no or maybe?
Scatter corn around the pen.
You and me and baby.

Yes,
    We'll feed the speckled hen
    Scratching in the dew.
    Then she'll lay two speckled eggs,
    One for each of you.

Momma, will you ride the foal?
Yes or no or maybe?
Coat as black as dusty coal.
Ride with me and baby.

No,
   We will not ride the foal,
   For foals are babies, too.
   I'll find a strong and dappled horse
   To ride with both of you.

Momma, will you dress the cat?
Yes or no or maybe?
Dress her in a lacy hat.
Dress her like our baby.

Maybe,
    We will dress the cat,
    If she won't run away.
    Then I'll help you with your shoes
    So you can run and play.

Momma, will you milk the cow?
Yes or no or maybe?
We would like some sweet milk now.
Milk for me and baby.

Yes,
   I'll milk the spotted cow.
   I'll fill the bucket up.
   Then you'll drink a glass of milk
   While baby drinks a cup.

Momma, will you catch a wren?
Yes or no or maybe?
Put him in a cage, and then
He will sing for baby.

No,
   We will not catch a wren,
   For wild things should fly free.
   But I will sing a song for you,
   And you sing one for me.

Momma, will you pluck the goose?
Yes or no or maybe?
Pull out feathers that are loose.
Some for me and baby.

Maybe,
    I will pluck the goose
    That sits beneath the willows,
    Then capture all the softest down
    To put inside your pillows.

Momma, will you wash the pig?
Yes or no or maybe?
In the tub! He's not too big.
Wash him with our baby.

Yes,
   We'll wash the little pig,
   But not in baby's tub!
   First we'll wash our baby's cheeks
   And give your knees a scrub.

Momma, will you fetch the pup?
Yes or no or maybe?
Hold him close to cuddle up
With you and me and baby.

Maybe,
   I will fetch the pup,
   Which likes my children's kisses.
   But I will watch and quickly take
   Any that he misses.

Momma, will you catch the mouse?
Yes or no or maybe?
In her nest beneath the house.
Show it to our baby.

No,
   I will not catch the mouse,
   For night is quickly creeping.
   Close your eyes and rest your head,
   For even mice are sleeping.

*Shhhh . . .*

*For Linda Smith and Melanie Cecka, with love*
—D. C.

*For Heather, Teresa, Bethany, and family*
—S. J. & L. F.

VIKING
Published by Penguin Group
Penguin Young Readers Group, 345 Hudson Street, New York, New York 10014, U.S.A.
Penguin Books Ltd, 80 Strand, London WC2R 0RL, England
Penguin Books Australia Ltd, 250 Camberwell Road, Camberwell, Victoria 3124, Australia
Penguin Books Canada Ltd, 10 Alcorn Avenue, Toronto, Ontario, Canada M4V 3B2
Penguin Group (NZ), cnr Airborne and Rosedale Roads, Albany, Auckland 1310, New Zealand

First published in 2004 by Viking, a division of Penguin Young Readers Group

1   3   5   7   9   10   8   6   4   2

LIBRARY OF CONGRESS CATALOGING-IN-PUBLICATION DATA
Chaconas, Dori, date-
Momma, will you? / written by Dori Chaconas ; illustrated by Steve Johnson and Lou Fancher.
p. cm.
Summary: As they make their way around the farm, a young boy asks his mother a series of questions
about the animals found there, to which she answers "yes," "no," or "maybe" and explains why.
ISBN 0-670-05907-2 (hardcover)
Special Markets ISBN 978-0-670-06015-3
Not for Resale
[1. Domestic animals—Fiction. 2. Animals—Fiction. 3. Farm life—Fiction. 4. Questions and answers—Fiction.
5. Stories in rhyme.] I. Johnson, Steve, date- ill. II. Fancher, Lou, ill. III. Title.
PZ8.3.C345Mom 2004 [E]—dc22 2004004085

Set in Stone Informal
Manufactured in China
Book design by Lou Fancher